For Edward & Scarlett
G.S.

For Timothy, with love
A.C.

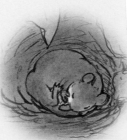

Bloomsbury Publishing, London, Berlin and New York

First published in Great Britain in 2009 by Bloomsbury Publishing Plc
36 Soho Square, London, W1D 3QY

Text copyright © Gillian Shields 2009
Illustrations copyright © Anna Currey 2009
The moral right of the author and illustrator has been asserted

A CIP catalogue record of this book is available from the British Library

ISBN 978 0 7475 8848 1

Printed in China by WKT Printing Co.Ltd

1 3 5 7 9 10 8 6 4 2

All papers used by Bloomsbury Publishing are natural, recyclable products made
from wood grown in well-managed forests. The manufacturing processes
conform to the environmental regulations of the country of origin

www.bloomsbury.com/childrens

When the World Is Ready for Bed

Gillian Shields

Illustrated by Anna Currey

BLOOMSBURY

LONDON BERLIN NEW YORK

When the world
Is ready for bed,
The sky grows dark,
The sun glows red.

The little flowers
Shut their eyes,
The night birds sing
Their lullabies.

Supper's ready
In the pot –
Come and eat it
While it's hot.

Now clear the room
And tidy up.
There's a toy
And here's a cup.

Let's talk about
The things you've done –
All the laughter,
All the fun.

Clean your teeth
And brush your hair.
Fold your clothes
Upon the chair.

Close the curtains,
Sleepyhead.
Find your blanket,
Cuddle Ted.

Pictures, stories,
One last look
At the tales
In one last book.

The lamp glows softly
On the stairs.
It's time for kisses,
Hugs and prayers . . .

. . . And look! A star
Is shining bright,
To guard you
In the dreaming night.

Today has nearly
Slipped away.
Tomorrow brings
Another day.

Always lovely,
Always new,
Tomorrow's waiting –
Just for you.